# My Fantasy Princess

**Robert Anderson**

Robert Anderson



ISBN: 978-1-966642-38-1

# Dedication

This book is dedicated to the Princess in this story. She alone would know if she was real or only in my fantasy.

Robert Anderson

# Acknowledgment

There is no proof my Fantasy Princess was real except in my memory of her.

# **Table of Contents**

# About the Author

God has blessed me with a very interesting life. I hope by sharing some of my life stories, my readers will see Christ in my life stories. My memory is being affected by a series of mini-strokes in my brain. I have been enjoying writing about some of my wonderful memories to document them before they are all gone.

# Introduction

Not long after I was diagnosed with my mother's dementia, I started to plan for my journey. I started to write stories about the wonderful life God had blessed me with before they were gone. All my stories proclaim the love and forgiveness of God.

Reading this story, it will be obvious that I was not a saint. I have had an interesting and exciting life with my Lord Jesus. I walked with Him on the mountain, and He carried me through some dark and sinful valleys.

God has been there with me through the dark, sinful periods of despair with alcohol, drugs, sex, and unholy times. Only to forgive me and use those experiences to relate to those caught in Satan's traps.

This is one of the oxymoron stories that is full of contradictions. How could telling a story about such an unholy relationship show God's love and mercy? As humans, we have all sinned and are in need of His forgiveness.

I wrote this story years after my diagnosis. My memory of the details was questionable back then. Now, 5 years later, my memory of the details is almost gone. Still, it brings back a wonderful, sweet memory of a beautiful Filipino I once dated for a month.

This is a story about a love affair I had with a Filipino call girl from San Francisco. People who think they know me would be shocked to read this story. It may sound so unbelievable and a complete fantasy. To think such a religious Christian man would have such a sordid affair with a call girl is just absurd. Turns out she was a Pacific Island princess just looking for a safe place to hide.

This is how I chose to remember it five years ago.

# Chapter 1

# How You Met Lee

You met Lee sometime in the middle of the eight years between your second and third wives. You had a few girlfriends and even a lover or two, but nothing was working out. Your journey with God has been so fulfilling and full of His blessings. You were at another crisis point in your life.

Your relationships with so many teenage girls became the breaking point with your second wife. She had not understood what it meant to marry a counselor for a Christian youth group for outside and troubled teenagers.

The truth was that even your group leader was concerned about all the runaways sleeping over at your apartment. It was time to break everything off and find some peace and refreshment in your soul. You had poured your heart and love out to so many that you were empty and in need of God's rest.

You took only your biological daughter and moved far away, back in with your parents. A middle-aged man is living with his parents and his teenage daughter. Separated from your second wife and not having any luck finding the right woman.

I don't know if you were all that lonely, but you decided to look into an online mail-order wife. Only one thing was certain: you could pick out the most beautiful bride, and she would be easy-going and pleasant. I blame it on your uncle Jimmy for wanting a Filipino wife. He told you stories about his housekeeper when he was in the Army stationed at Clark Air Base in the Philippines.

I don't remember him telling you if she was pretty or not, but I do know he really liked her very much. He told you of his drunken parties with his buddies from the army and how pleasant she was always to him. I don't remember if they were lovers or not, but sex in the Philippines was pretty easy to come by if you had money. He told you how friendly and nice she was to all the girls he brought home and how she cared for him.

With my uncle's experience and a little investigating, I learned why they call the Philippines the wife tree. Filipino women run most of the households in the Philippines. In general, they are stronger than their husbands. Most Filipino men like it just that way. Nanay takes care of everything needed to run the family. So, they often come in a very tiny, beautiful package. Most often, my Catholic mom and I love going to church and praying.

It started out so straightforward and upright. You were a middle-aged Christian man living with your teenage daughter. The bar scene was not right for you. God knows you spent enough time looking for the right woman to fulfill all of your dreams in both churches and bars. This was going to be the answer.

I don't remember how, but you got on a website for foreign women looking for American husbands. It looked pretty good. That is, it did not seem to be a pure sex-for-hire website. Remember, back in the 80s, your computer was still running a DOS operating system before Windows.

I don't remember, but I know it cost a lot of money just to get a membership to view the women available. Thanks to your uncle, you filtered your choice to women from the Philippines. You thought, what the hell? Even if this was just another sex-for-hire website, you could have a great time with a high-class call girl without even going to the Philippines.

You thumbed through page by page of the most beautiful young Filipinas you had ever seen. You made your choice and paid the fee to get her phone number to call her directly. After looking at all those beautiful women and reading their suggestive bios, you really started to get more excited and think more about a call girl than a bride.

You got up enough courage and made that phone call. Five minutes after hearing that timid little voice answer the phone, you knew you had to meet her. She told you she was in trouble and needed your help. For all you know, it was all part of the act to get more money. The more she talked, the more convincing she became. I don't remember what she told you on that first phone call, but there was nothing going to stop you from seeing her. She said the membership plus the phone call, I could pay another fee to take her out to dinner.

Do you remember the feelings you had as you made that long drive from Fort Bragg to San Francisco? Was this girl really in trouble, or was this going to be the greatest one-night fling in your life?

It was a nice, high-rise apartment near UC San Francisco. You were shaking like a leaf when you rang the doorbell. A middle-aged woman answered and asked you to come into the front room. There was a man sitting on a couch and a couple of other girls in the next room. The woman started to ask questions, and you knew you were in the wrong place. This was not my date's apartment but more like a whore house.

Whatever, you were committed. You had the money in your pocket, she had told you it would cost to take her out for dinner. The woman asked you if you wanted to meet Lee. That's why I'm here, you said. Then she walked into the room, and your heart started pounding. The crummy mugshot on the website did her great injustice. She was stunningly beautiful in a short, tight little black dress. Your eyes went from her perfectly shaped legs up to her tiny waist. She had perfectly shaped, high, firm breasts and a sweet angel face looking at you with mysterious, dark eyes. She had long dark hair and a sweet smile on her full Filipino lips as she sat down beside you on the couch. You reached out and held her trembling hand.

The man said," This one is special; she is still a virgin." She is running out of time and needs to get married soon. Bring her back from dinner a virgin, or don't bring her back at all; we will find you. You knew exactly what that meant.

Lee looked into your eyes as the man was giving you instructions. Don't remember what she said, but there was a lot of chemistry and feelings going on between you. You sat there, motionless on the couch next to Lee, staring into your eyes. It was like private communication between your spirits while holding hands for the very first time.

You were so confused with all the conflicting emotions going through your head. Your body was still excited from watching this sexy goddess walk into the room in her short, tight, low-cut dress. Still, her almond-shaped, dark eyes were interrogating your soul. Your body wanted to look away from her probing eyes to look at her beautiful, generous breasts. But your spirit couldn't stop looking into her mysterious eyes.

Stop right here.

This is a story to tell your older self after your memory of this moment has left the building.

Remember what you did next. I will have to remind you that you were no stranger to trusting God to lead you to help a number of terrified teenage girls in trouble. You were a counselor for a Christian teenage mission years before. Looking into her terrified eyes, she became another frightened girl that God wanted you to trust.

Looking back now, it was the first contact between both your physical bodies and your spirits. You gave the man the money, and you walked out together holding hands. I will have her home before midnight, and the door will be closed behind you. As the elevator door closed, she fell into your arms and began crying uncontrollably.

# Chapter 2

# First Dinner

Can't remember what was said or how long it took to get to the restaurant. Sorry, I don't remember all the details, but it was like out of a Hollywood romance movie. As I write this story to you, I can still see the image of this goddess sitting across the table from you. It felt like you were looking through the lens of a commercial Air-Flex movie camera on the set filming a scene for a Hollywood movie.

Lee was simply a gorgeous little Filipina lady. Her high cheekbones and round little innocent face. She had the most captivating, big, dark almond-shaped eyes. Beautiful straight white teeth and an intoxicating smile. Her lips had red, glossy lipstick; they were thick, full, Filipino, and you loved to look at them as she talked to you across the table.

You could not help noticing how the low-cut tight dress was exposing her lush, generous breasts. She obviously had no need for a bra, and her nipples were stressing points on her thin black dress. She was not the professional sex worker the image was projecting. She was timid and very shy, just like she was on the phone. You had seen that same look of terror in those frightened eyes back at the apartment.

You reached across the table, held her hands, and prayed to Jesus to bless this trembling little angel. The tears swelled up in her eyes, and she began to cry. I don't remember everything you prayed for, but she seemed to be much more trusting after that prayer.

She said she was looking for a nice man she could trust. All the other men she had met through the foreign bride agency were just looking for sex. She thought you might be someone she could trust because she could see the love of God in your eyes. She didn't understand it, but she said she felt safe and she could trust you.

She told you the story of how she got into this situation.

Her godfather had a contract with these marriage agency people. They were to let her select a suitable husband in person. Secretly get married in Vegas and fly right back home all in 30 days. It was supposed to be a sham wedding right from the start. He had paid enough money to get around the INS rules and still be a legal marriage. She agreed to do this, knowing she would be safe because no one would cross her godfather with all of his underworld connections both in the States and in Manila.

Suppose she could find the right guy to go along with a secret marriage in name only. Take a few pictures in Las Vegas, and no one will ever have to know about it. She said her godfather would make it right for anyone willing to go along. He told her to find someone nice in case all he wants in payment is sex and a housekeeper. You have several cousins in California who might love to fulfill your marriage obligations for a couple of years.

She looked at you with those sweet eyes and asked if you might be interested. All the other men she had been introduced to were nothing like what she was looking for.

You knew you were in serious trouble by this time. You confessed to her that you were still legally married and that you could not legally marry her. Then she started to cry, and you felt so rotten inside. She stopped crying and told you how good that was to hear and how happy she was. You were so puzzled, you did not know what to say.

The only way she could get away from her handlers back at the agency was to get married. They only get paid when she gets married. They told her that you were her last chance. They would be making the selection for her if you didn't work out. Everything was going wrong back home in the Philippines. Her marriage handlers had lost contact with her godfather.

Marcos had just declared martial law in the Philippines, and her godfather was now missing, and nobody knew where he was hiding. Now, she was being treated just like all the other girls back at the agency. She knew she would be forced to marry and live with anyone they selected for at least 18 months. A year and a half of sex and a housekeeper was worth the price tag.

Under your breath, you thought, that was just what you had in mind, you dirty old man. Somehow, you believed her story, and you were sure she was really in trouble, and you wanted to help her. You asked her what you could do to help her. She said, Marry me and take me away from that awful place, or there may be another option.

Then she told you more about her family and her boyfriend back home in Manila. Their families had been planning a big wedding for years until all the trouble came up in the Philippines. She was in love with her boyfriend, and they both cried when she parted for a 30-day vacation to the States. She had agreed to this quick sham wedding just to give her parents the option to get out of the country as fast as possible. Now, all she really wanted was to get back home, but there was no escape from her handlers.

She told you that one other girl was given a 30-day pre-marriage trial if the money was put up front. She told you that if you really wanted to help her, she had the money to pay them for a 30-day trial period, and she could stay with you until she got on an airplane back home.

Her 30-day tourist visa had already expired, and she was worried about immigration finding her. Her parents had pulled enough strings to get her on a flight back to Manila somehow at the end of the month. First, she had to escape from her handlers.

With all the trouble back home, they wanted to complete their contract with her godfather before he disappeared altogether.

The deal was simple: pay the money upfront and keep in contact for 30 days. At the end of the 30 days, either she can produce a legal marriage certificate or pay to get her back. They got their final payment when they could prove a legal marriage was complete.

Before dinner was over, she had transformed into a calm, controlled businesswoman. Still sweet and innocent, but seemed in control of the situation.

She told you just what to say and what not to say when you got back to the apartment. Her vacation was over, and she needed to get back to work.

You knew you had lost control, and there was no stopping things now. She was so gorgeous and sweet and innocent, and she was really in trouble. No question that she was intelligent and crafty enough to pull this off, if you were willing to go along.

I don't remember much about all that happened when you got her back to the apartment. I know you had to let them make a copy of your driver's license and sign some documents.

This time, the environment was even more threatening than it was before dinner. You gave them the money (that Lee had given you) and promised to return before the end of the month. It was clear to you; these people were not the kind of folks you didn't do exactly what they said.

Another man came into the room and took Lee by the arm into the other room. A few minutes later, she came back dressed in tight jeans and a sweater and holding a small suitcase. It was obvious she had been crying, and you were afraid to ask her why. The in-control businesswoman had turned back into a frightened little kitten again. You could feel her shaking when you reached out to take her trembling hand.

The moment you stepped into the elevator, it was like a giant sigh of relief for both of you. You wrapped your arms around her, and she began to cry as she told you what that man had done to her in the bedroom. She continued to cry as you put your arms around her and walked her to your car.

# Chapter 3

# First Night Together

Remember, you were looking for a mail-order bride for a reason. You were lonely and tired of looking for your soulmate in bars and churches. You had taken this chance, not knowing if it was the right thing to do. You were lonely and longed to be in a physical relationship.

Before dinner, it was all lust and desire for sex that brought you to her. Now, God had placed yet another helpless little sister for you to show her God's love and protection. In your dirty, lustful mind, you had already made a reservation at a hotel in Santa Cruz. Just in case the dinner went as you had hoped.

Without saying much, you drove her that hour's drive to the Dream Inn resort overlooking the Santa Cruz Beach and Boardwalk, plus a great view across the Monterey Bay.

She sat as far away from you as possible against her car door. Crying and saying thank you, Kuya, over and over, all the way across the Santa Cruz Mountains to the hotel. She took a shower, put on some night clothes, and climbed into bed while you took your shower.

She lay on her side at the edge of the bed with her back toward you. You slid into bed and held her trembling body next to you. Without saying a word, you cuddled up next to her and put your arms around her. She didn't have to say it. I'm sure she was still terrified of what that man had done to her in the bedroom.

You gently held her until she cried herself to sleep. By this time, you knew she had been telling you the truth all along, and she was not your sex toy for the night. She was, in fact, a real lady in serious trouble, and it was your job to protect and care for her. Later that night, she woke up.

She had rolled over and was facing you with her head on your shoulder and her leg wrapped around yours. She woke up and looked at you, right in your eyes, and smiled with such a sweet look. Never in your life can you remember anything like that moment. You had fantasized for years about how it would be to have sex with a beautiful movie star like this. Your expectations of a wild, crazy night of ecstasy with a professional call girl paled in comparison with what you were feeling. Sex with a call girl would be over in minutes, and she would be gone. This was something totally different and far more satisfying, and had lasted all night. This beautiful angel was still there, lying next to you, and you thought this was only a dream. You don't remember a word she said, but you do know they were like honey dripping from those beautiful Filipino lips. She snuggled up even closer and placed her sweet head against your neck.

She was still trembling inside from all that was going on in that sweet little head of hers. In the morning, she called her mother back in Manila. You had no idea what they were talking about because they were talking in Tagalog. You do know there was a lot of sobbing and emotion, and she seemed not to be so frightened after the call. She handed you the phone, and you were able to talk to her mother in English. I don't remember much of what she told you, but some feelings still remain about that call. You knew you had a precious gem in your care, and you promised her mother to keep her safe. She must have told her mother that you did not try to have sex with her that night and that you were being a gentleman. You must have told her you would take good care of her daughter, like she was your very own little daughter in trouble. After breakfast, you went for a walk on the beach, holding hands, not like lovers but more like a daddy and his frightened little girl. You told her you would be taking good care of her and never worry about sex between you. You took her for a couple of rides on the Boardwalk, and everything seemed to lighten up. You ate hot dogs and French fries under that famous boardwalk on the beach. From then on, she was going to be your little girl, and you would show her your Christian love and a safe place in your arms. Her voice was changing from being a frightened, scared woman to becoming a little girl in the hands of a loving daddy. What do daddies do with their little girls? They go to Disneyland.

You got a room in the Disneyland hotel on the 6th floor overlooking the park for 3 nights. I would like to report that your most extreme pleasure was watching her run and jump from one thrilling ride to the other; in her excitement was your best memory. That was not all you remember about your stay in

Disneyland. No, it was not the dinners with the Disney characters or the laughter and fun she was having. What I remember now most to tell you is the sweet, long nights in bed, cuddled up so close to her. Your arms wrapped around her, and you kissed the back of her head.

It was obvious that she had never slept in the middle between her mommy and daddy like all your daughters had done. She was so appreciative that it was so safe and warm next to you. You could feel the fear of being so close fading away with every passing night. By the time it was time to leave Disneyland, she was getting so close and familiar with sleeping next to you. As I write this story for you, I remember those days at Disneyland when she was just your little girl, and you were just her loving daddy.

Things were really changing for her. From being so frightened out of her mind to having such a good time. It was true; Disneyland was the happiest place on earth. Looking back now, this is where she made her big mistake. Little girls tell their daddies about everything, like their friends, family, and, most of all, boyfriends. She told you several stories about home.

They lived in a big house in a very nice neighborhood just outside of Manila. She did not say, but it was clear she had maids and housekeepers and drivers to take her anywhere she wanted to go. She went to the finest Catholic schools and graduated from a very good university in Manila. They had a summer house in Baggio, high up in the cool mountains in northern Luzon.

Vacations in Japan because her father was part Japanese and still had some family there. Her mother's uncle was her wealthy godfather, and she was very close to him. Sometimes, her godfather would take her and some girlfriends from college for overnight trips on his yacht. You could see why he would like to have 3 or 4 beautiful girls like her along for the ride. It was on one of those calm, peaceful sailing trips with her godfather where she could be alone with her boyfriend.

The stories about her boyfriend were probably the most important factor that stuck in your stupid brain. He was from another high-society family, and they were to be married someday after everything settled down. She told you that she loved him and how he cried when she left on vacation to the States for a month. He did not know her real plan to secretly get married and come back home. It was all supposed to be a secret.

After college, her godfather got her a job at a bank, and she soon became an officer. Not long after that, she became the branch manager. Then everything was going south, and there was real trouble for her whole family. Her godfather told them he could arrange a quick sham wedding, and she could file a petition to get her family moved to the States if things got really bad.

He told her he knew some people who could line up some possible men in the States for you to meet in person before getting married in name only, and fly back home. You would have to like the guy, and he must be trusted to keep his mouth shut. A few pictures in Las Vegas, and he would be cared for as long as he wanted. Then, a quiet divorce

She also told you the backup plan. Suppose you don't find the perfect guy for you. Then pick the best one you can. You can tell him I have several young "nieces" in America. I could send one of them to sleep with him and keep his house for a couple of years. Just get married fast and get back home. I will take care of everything.

Well, it's a good thing you couldn't give her that fake "name only" wedding. You were still married. You had never even filed for a divorce. Now, there was so much trouble back home, all everyone wanted was to get her safely back home to Manila.

The long and wonderful pillow talks you had went both ways. You told her your redneck stories about where you were from and all the wives and girlfriends you had. It really was like Daddy telling his new little adopted daughter all about her new daddy. The same goes for her, like telling Daddy about all the things she loved, including the love of her life and her real boyfriend back home.

After Disneyland, you took a ferry to the island of Santa Catalina, just off the coast from Long Beach. This was familiar to you because you spent a week there with your son and his beautiful, sweet girlfriend before. She loved it so much. Shopping in all those little boutiques and walking on the beach. You rented a golf cart and drove around the island. Dinner watching the evening sunset from the famous Avalon Pavilion restaurant, and breakfast at the open-air cafe next to the beach. Just like Disneyland, it was the long, sweet night sleeping next to this goddess that should give you so much joy to remember.

You left LA and headed north to Santa Barbara for your next night with your little fairy princess. Stopped off at the Santa Monica Pier for a ride on that famous Ferris wheel.

Ate lunch at Malibu Beach café under the warm sunshine and waves hitting the beach. She was constantly looking out for movie stars. You did not care that you were with the most attractive lady in the whole place. You told her after lunch that everyone was looking at her. Your best guess is they had never seen a real, live Filipino princess like that, looking just like a movie star they recognized.

# Chapter 4

# Crossing that Line

You pulled into the beachside cottage in Santa Barbra just about dark. She was hungry, so you took her out to Brophy's on the pier for dinner. You got a window seat overlooking the lights from the sailboats in the marina and in the harbor. Looking at her eyes, looking back into yours, things began to change for both of you. That was the romantic moment I want you to remember forever. The image of such a gorgeous, lovely lady looking into your eyes like that is the thing wars are fought for.

Our conversation shifted from talking with Daddy to his happy little girl to hardly any talking at all. We both just stared into each other's eyes for a very long time without speaking. This time, it was more than her beautiful, almond-shaped, dark eyes looking back. There was something else going on between you two. No, it wasn't just her movie star eyebrows and perfectly curled eyelashes with the perfect soft eye makeup to make her eyes shine. It was something coming from inside her eyes that was telling you that she may be falling in love.

She gently put her hands on the back of both your hands on the table. Her tender, light touch as she rubbed the back of your hands was different somehow. It felt so exciting, more like being touched by a lover as she continued to look into your eyes. Another long romantic walk on the beach after dinner.

Before bed, she called her mother and talked for a very long time. You did not understand a word they said, but it was a lot. Then she handed you the phone again to talk to her mother. You found out where Lee got her business head from. Mom, or should I say "the general," told me just how grateful she was that you were protecting her daughter. She told you that Lee was very happy with you, and she was looking forward to spending the month with you until her return home.

She told you they were leaving Manila and going up into the mountains until things got better in the city. She also told you that she would make it worth your while if you saw that she got home safe. There was no saying no to Mommy (her godfather's niece). The direct threats from the marriage agency were nothing. Momma talked clearly, straight from her heart, and meant every word she said. She said all that with the sweetness of such a loving mother, you felt the love for her daughter in her voice, and you accepted the challenge with joy.

You hung up and did not have a clue what to say, so you just went to bed. She turned off the lights and crawled into bed next to you, just like all the other nights. Snuggled up like before, you put your arms around her and tried to go to sleep. Sometime later that night, she raised her head, and her warm, moist lips touched yours. You knew you would never have initiated anything, so you knew it was all her idea.

If you could possibly ever forget the feeling of that moment, then you don't remember the dozens of teenage girls who had called you daddy. Never in your life ever thought would you ever think of crossing that line with any of them. However, Lee was not a teenager. She was a 20-something goddess, and you were in your 40s. No other way to explain it was like being kissed by an angel straight out of heaven.

You fumbled and asked her what she was doing. "Honey, your mother thinks I am your daddy, and you are my little girl," you said or something like that. At the very least, you were more like a paid bodyguard. There is no kissing allowed. "As long as I go back home a virgin, they don't need to know how much fun I had," she said. She straight out asked you if you would be her boyfriend without having sex until she goes home.

You thought for a long, hard moment. What were you getting into? Before you could think, this can't happen. She kissed you again. This time, it was longer and softer, much gentler and sweeter. It felt like you were kissing the very first girl that you had ever kissed.

Seriously, so many of the same emotions and feelings, just like your first kiss with the 14-year-old Diane, your first girlfriend. Awkward, not knowing just what to do to each other or where to touch each other. Lee was acting confused and excited all at once. More like a teenager doing something she knew was wrong.

You felt like you were about to commit the unpardonable sin and become intimate with a woman half your age. The tension between you grew to a boiling point as you continued to look into each other's eyes.

What about your boyfriend back home? Well, as long as I go home, and I am still a virgin, nobody has to know I had a boyfriend to enjoy my stay in California with. She said she had other boyfriends before, without having sex with them. You said yes, but you were not sleeping with them. No, but I have already been sleeping with you without sex. Besides, she said those romantic dinners and walks on the beach were having a romantic effect on her.

Can't we just be good friends and kiss both? She asked. Momma says I can have a boyfriend while I'm here as long as I come home a virgin. Can I be your girlfriend until I go home, she asked.

Now, you are not the smartest guy in town, but you are not a complete idiot. There you were, sitting cross-legged on the bed, facing the gorgeous little woman looking into your eyes, asking to be your girlfriend for a month. What could possibly go wrong?

The feel of her warm, smooth skin on her shoulders as you pulled her close. You looked down into a young, beautiful Filipina face, smiling back at you. Yes, you kissed her, or did she kiss you? There was no way to tell. It was so enjoyable that neither of you wanted it to end. Come to think of it, you made out like two teenagers all that night.

After Santa Barbra, you drove her up the California coast on the coastal highway one. This time, you were holding hands as you drove the twisted and winding highway. You had driven that beautiful coast highway before with other girls in your Corvette. Not that the other girls were not pretty; they all were. You would not trade this ride with Nicole Kidman, your favorite sexy movie star, for the Filipina goddess sitting next to you.

You could not tell if it was the breathtaking view of the coastline or you she was looking at. Whatever it was, she was either falling in love or really liking the ride. You can put a beautiful woman's face in a magazine, but you can't put the joy of that moment in her eyes. You taught her how to change gears in your sports car as you held her hand on the shifter.

Stopped for lunch on the secluded beach at Shell Beach. It was only fish and chips from the bar in Pismo, but what a picnic on the beach that was. The pure white sand in the warm sun, kissing a Playboy Playmate on a blanket. The tiny bathing suit she bought at Catalina was drawing a lot of attention.

You stayed on the coast highway to San Louis Obispo and just drove past the Morrow Bay Rock. You were not in a hurry, so you gave in to her request to visit the Hurst Castle. You drove the Monterey loop so she could see the Pebble Beach golf course. She said she was still full from the picnic, so you did not eat at Cannery Row as you had planned. Then, around Monterey Bay, back to Santa Cruz, where you spent that first night together.

You got a room at the Dream Inn again, only a different room. The room was not the only difference this time. There was something more than just physical going on between you and her. A normal person would just say you were just romantically falling in love this time. Not you. You really believed there was something more, something spiritual going on between you. The scary thing is she was acting like she was falling in love, too.

It wasn't all just making out like kids on holiday from college or even sleeping together, all cuddled up every night. It was the long, sweet talks, cuddled up on the hotel couch. Laughing and kissing and eating just to start laughing all over again.

Then, there was the intellectual side of Lee. She gave you a compelling argument on the benefits of a close physical relationship without sex if you were willing to accept it. I must admit it would be very nice to go to sleep kissing her lips instead of the back of her head.

The next morning, it was off to see the San Francisco cable cars. You had lunch at the top of the spinning Hyatt restaurant at the foot of Market Street. Then you took a bike taxi to Pier 39 and Fisherman's Wharf along the embarcadero. You took her up to the top of Coit Tower to see the panoramic view of the entire San Francisco Bay. The Golden Gate Bridge and Alcatraz are to your left, and the Bay Bridge and Oakland are to your right. Her favorite was the drive down the steep and twisting flower garden of Lombard Street just before leaving the city.

Crossed the Golden Gate Bridge and up to the Marin Headlands to view the city from high, overlooking the bridge from the north. Looking down on the bridge, with San Francisco shining like a gem behind it. Alcatraz Island, with the Oakland hills behind that. Golden Gate Park and the Presidio Army base are just right of the bridge.

Heading north, we drove through the Muir Woods old-growth redwood trees past Stinson Beach to Bodega Bay. Another romantic rustic motel overlooking the harbor. Dinner by the fishing boat dock was like another movie set.

The noisy seagulls and the smelly fish boats could not dim the sparkle in her eyes. The sunset's warm rays, lighting her intoxicating face, were having a profound effect on your brain. It was well beyond just physical between you. You were feeling more and more comfortable telling each other secrets and dreams. Knowing you only had a short time together.

It wasn't all a Filipino drama with just tears and tragedy. You spent more time laughing than you did kissing. She had more jokes and tricks to keep you both laughing. Sometimes, she would sing along with the radio. What a beautiful voice she had. You loved to hear her sing along with Barbra Streisand on the radio.

It was another long talk with her mother back home and a short talk with you, too. You were so embarrassed and ashamed because you were not a very good father figure to her daughter, as you said. You were beginning to have very romantic thoughts about your little princess.

Each time you tried to tell Lee what you were feeling was all wrong; she found new ways to distract you from any such silly ideas. Just a few words from those sweet Filipino lips, and it was all just going to be okay. It just felt like things were getting out of your control, but you did not know what to do about it.

# Chapter 5

# Bringing Her Home

Your relationship had grown to a point where it was only logical you bring her to the safety of your home back in the north woods. Your parents were strict, conservative Baptist Christians. Even so, Lee would not be the first girlfriend you had brought home to Momma. You knew your folks would love to help you hide her for a month.

On the final leg to Fort Bragg, you had to pass the Point Arena lighthouse.

The picturesque village of Mendocino. You did stop at the vista point to look at Mendocino from across Big River Bay. It is like a snapshot in time taken back in the 1800s. Settled by Spain after the Russians and Mexico, this old-world village is unique. For now, we just drove through it on our way to your mother's house, just 15 miles north.

You parked in front of your parents' simple, small, 2-bedroom old house and expected some negative response from your new girlfriend. There was nothing; she bounced out of the car and almost skipped, holding your hand up to the front door. From her mansion back home in Manila to this simple little cluttered house must have been a shock. Nothing like that; she almost became one of the family from the very first hug she gave your dad.

Your mother loved her from the very start; then again, your mother loved all your wives and girlfriends you had ever brought home. Right away, your mother told you that you needed to get married. I don't remember all the reasons why, but she was sure you were done looking around. Your mother must have found out you were looking for a mail-order bride or something.

Remember, you were living there with your real biological teenage daughter. She was in on several failures in your romantic relationships. What? Even she liked your new girlfriend. She knew Lee was way too pretty and too young to ever be a real threat to her daddy.

This is where the story changes again. Once more, you slept next to her in your loft, and your daughter slept in hers. The next day, at breakfast, more and more gushing from your mother and dad over your new girlfriend. You knew you had lost control, and everyone was talking about you and Lee. Another very long talk with her mother on the phone back in Manila, and more talks alone with your mother.

You had converted your mother's craft house in the backyard into a small studio for you and your daughter to sleep in. It was pretty nice inside with a fresh new soft carpet and a small kitchenette, and a bathroom. You had built two sleeping lofts, one at each end of the studio. It had large skylight windows over the beds at each end. Well, they were not beds; they were just king-sized mattresses on the floor in each sleeping loft.

Your daughter was spending the night with a girlfriend, and you were alone with Lee in the studio that night. It was just like before you went to bed and were in the middle of the sweetest kissing and romantic embrace, when she sat up on her knees and slipped off her T-shirt. The soft blue night light from the skylight above the bed lit those beautiful breasts for the very first time. She took both your hands and placed them softly on her breast. Your lights went out for a few seconds. After you came back to earth, you had difficulty figuring out what just happened.

Her mother must have said something to her. Not even Lee would be so bold without some kind of okay from the general back home.

Your relationship with her changed that night with an explosion of ecstasy and emotion. She lay down beside your trembling body and cuddled up next to you in only her panties and whispered into your ear. My mother said as long as I came home still a virgin, there were lots of things like that we could do. What are you talking about? Is this your mother's idea? Lee had been talking about having that kind of sex for a number of days, but never thought her mother would be any part of it.

The first time was all over before you knew what was happening. The second time was still over in seconds, but it was clear she did not know what she was doing. This was the first time she had ever done anything like that to a man. She was clumsy and fumbled, but her touch felt so incredible. She lay with her beautiful bare breast on your chest and began kissing you like never before. She whispered in your ear; Please say you will divorce your wife and marry me.

Turns out things were getting even worse back in the Philippines. The general had changed the plan since her daughter was having such a wonderful time on vacation with you. Why not just change the original plan? Since they were hiding in the mountains, it may not be safe for her to come home yet.

A new plan from the general to get married in name only and file the petition to let her parents emigrate to the States whenever they needed to. Just remain on vacation with your secret boyfriend for a couple of years. Just come home as a virgin and get married again for real, like we planned.

Clearly, Lee was willing to pull out all the stops to get you to file for a divorce and committed to marrying her as soon as it was final.

Your mind had been blown apart, and you could not think of anything to say. You were losing all control and felt like you were being pulled apart inside. Let's talk about it in the morning after I stop shaking.

You were already skeptical about whether you could complete the task of keeping her safe for a month without falling completely in love with her. How could you possibly marry her and let her go in two years to return home?

She had confessed to her mother, back home, that you were her boyfriend, but she knew where to draw the line. What the general did not know was that things between you were already more than just physical. Now, throw in the element of sex, and there would be no stopping falling head over heels in love. We were already enjoying each other's company so much, and now you are actually lovers.

Any normal person would see nothing but stars and fireworks for just one more day with this beauty. Not you. What you saw was nothing but a contradiction between extreme ecstasy and an atomic bomb blast at the end. You did not care about the words coming out of her pretty mouth. She had already told you in Disneyland how much she loved her boyfriend back home and how much she wanted to marry him and have his babies.

You knew you could never give her the life she was used to and deserved, and children were out of the question. You felt you would have God's blessing and support to carry you over, saying goodbye in 3 weeks, but there was no way you could survive saying goodbye in 2 years. Besides, you did not believe she could say goodbye then, either. Being her knight in shining armor for 3 more weeks was one thing, but to be her lover for 2 years was out of the question.

You stayed awake most of that night, coming up with a plan. For years, you had still been using the line that you were still in love with your existing second wife as an excuse to break off relationships. You were good at it for a number of reasons. Not only was there so much practice, but there was also a bit of the truth in it, making it much easier to pull it off.

Lee would be fighting a losing battle trying to get you to let her give up the life back home she described so well while in Disneyland. Back then, she was your damsel in distress, and you could do anything to get her home safe. Now, you were already wanting her to stay forever, but at what a hard cost for her.

The next morning, you told her straight out that you would never marry her and that she had a date with the airline to go back home in 3 weeks. You gave her the story about still being in love with your second wife and lied about wanting to get back together after all the kids had grown up. She just smiled and said with a grin, We will see about that. Look at it this way: you had 3 weeks to show her the time of her life, and just maybe, she will get tired of you and want to go home.

I know you don't remember, but the next 3 weeks will be the greatest Playboy dream fantasy for you. It was more than 40 years ago, and my current memory of details is slipping away from me. So, I guess I will tell it as best I recall at this stage of your dementia.

# Chapter 6

# Mendocino Coast

After last night in the loft, everything changed. Even the general didn't want her daughter to come back to Manila just yet. They were still hiding in the mountains and just let Lee stay on an extended vacation with you. At the same time, she was still here anyway, so why not just get married while you wait for things to settle down? So why not just marry her in name only until the sham marriage is legal? Even if they could not count on her godfather's political help with the INS, it would still be a legal marriage to let them immigrate to the States.

What were you going to do? Marry her in name only for two years and let her go back to the Philippines to marry the love of her life. Back to her big mistake back in Disneyland. Her description of the true love she had for her real boyfriend back in Manila.

Most of my grandparents immigrated to America from Scandinavia. We Sweeds are known to be somewhat hardheaded. You had given your word to the general to safely escort her daughter to the airport at the end of the month. What the general doesn't know is how impossible it would be to let her go home in two years.

Your only recourse would be to distract her from the marriage thing as long as possible by showing her this wonderful Mendocino Coast where you were raised.

It was the spring of the year when you met Lee. Now, not only was spring in full swing so was your new love affair. To be so in love and in such a magnificent natural beauty of the Mendocino coast. You thought you could keep distracting her from the marriage thing for as long as possible.

You took her out to the Mendocino headlands overlooking the wild blue Pacific Ocean. The bluffs were covered in wildflowers this time of year. The sky was a dark blue with white, puffy clouds way out at sea. You spread out a blanket next to a patch of California Golden Poppies and ate another fantastic picnic lunch. Only this time it was more than wine and just kisses. She was pulling out all the big guns now to make you change your mind. Making out under the warm sun was much more intimate now after last night up in the sleeping loft.

Dinner with your parents and even more pressure from your folks before going to bed. This time, it was much harder to keep quiet enough not to disturb your daughter sleeping in the loft at the other end of the studio. Each day, you would take her to as many favorite spots as possible to show her the beautiful neck of the woods you grew up in.

As it turns out, you would have been the perfect man even for plan A. A clean, not bad-looking middle-aged man with a good, steady job, living way back in the woods with no reporters looking around. She could easily stay hidden from the Filipino gossip machine for a couple of years. Easy life with you for 2 years, and never gets noticed by anyone back home. Come back home still a virgin, marry her high-society boyfriend, and live happily ever after.

Assuming you have already forgotten this wonderful experience with Lee, you probably don't remember your history of taking photographs. Years before, you owned and ran a professional photography studio in Noyo Harbor just south of Fort Bragg. At the time you were dating Lee, you had taken several dozen weddings, including outdoor bridal portraits all over the Mendocino Coast. More than that, after closing the shop and going back to work for the power company, you accepted several dozen senior portraits each year. You knew all the romantic, cool places to take brides and sexy schoolgirls.

Before you took her to any of those places, you took her to your secret secluded beach just north of Glass Beach. It is only accessible at low tide, and there would be no possible people walking up on you past mid-tide. You had dreamed of taking a girl there since you were a young boy. You had a picnic on the beach, and she was learning a lot more and more about the art of making love to you.

Here you were, on your boyhood beach, where you sat as a boy and thought about girls. Noting the one hour of complete privacy on that beach before and after high tide. More than her magnificent body and sweet kisses, it was her tender, affectionate touch in that moment that should bring joy to remember.

You would lie together on the beach, and she would tell you how wonderful it would be if you married her. You would not have to work another day in your life once her parents got here. Until then, they could not wire any more money for fear it would be traced back to them. Remember, they were hiding for some reason. You knew this was true because her mother had wired you several thousand dollars to protect her and show her a good time in Disneyland.

I have already told you how beautiful she was. She had the body and face of a Playboy Playmate. Until now, I do not believe I have explained to you just how smart she was. Just like at your first dinner, you knew you could trust her to pull off that getaway from her scary handlers; she was now planning your whole life for you.

File for a divorce, bring a certified copy to the marriage agency to keep them off your butt. Get married 6 months after that, and her parents could find a way to buy a big house for all of us to live in. She was sure everything would be perfect.

To be honest, red flags and whistles were starting to go off in your head, just like you told your daughter. She always left out the part about her going back to the Philippines to marry her true love after two years. She was everything your uncle Jimmy said about the difference between the girls from the street and a proper Filipino wife.

Clearly, she could manage your household and still be the CEO of a large company. Talking about being my dream playmate, she would have been the perfect dream wife. Her mother's voice gave her loving advice, and her daughter's sweet lips on my face. How could I say goodbye at the end of a month, much less after two years?

I still had to be focused on the stories she told you about the love of her life back in Manila. She had painted such a grand picture of her wonderful life growing up in the Philippines. She told you the story about the time her godfather secretly arranged to have her boyfriend as a guest on a beautiful 3 days and 2 nights on his yacht.

Forget all that for now; let's just enjoy the next 3 weeks and cross that bridge when it comes. The next day, you took her back to Mendocino for breakfast at your favorite upstairs café overlooking the Big River Bay. Walked through the village, stopping at several hippie shops and art galleries. It was like a step back in time to the 1800s. Architecture and buildings look just like they did back then. You hung around to have dinner and see a live play at the art center.

The after-drinks at the old Seagull Inn were a little crazy. Many of your old photography clients were artists, and some were there, and you noticed a few of them, along with a bunch of pot-smoking hippies you also recognized. One of your old artist buddies sat down at your table and started to talk to your date. Next thing, he asked her to come up to his studio to pose for him. It was time for you to leave.

The next day, you went on a sweet and peaceful canoe ride up the Albion River. If you time it just right and rent the canoe at the turn of the incoming tide, you can float for miles without even paddling. There are no roads or houses for miles and miles, only pure nature on both sides of the slow-moving river. Beavers swim around their houses made from brush and logs. Two otters were playing on the south bank while a small deer was on the north side of the river. Lilly pads and frogs all along the banks. Wildflowers were everywhere, and kingfishers were flying overhead. Tall redwood, white fir, and pine trees on both sides. The smell of rhododendrons blooming back under the trees.

Lee was lying in the front of the canoe, looking up at the birds and trees passing over her head. You could not keep your eyes off her. It was such a pretty day surrounded by God's natural beauty, and in the middle of all that, there was Lee.

By now, she was beginning not to be so shy and was flirting with you from the front of the canoe. When the river got smaller and more intimate, so did Lee. Remember how hard it was to paddle and stare at the topless goddess five feet away from you?

You laughed as another couple passed, going down the river. You should have warned her they were coming around the bend. They both saw Lee's beautiful full breast as she was lying on her back at the front of the canoe. Lee covered herself with her arms and glared at you with intent to kill as they paddled by.

Beached the canoe near a meadow covered with tall grass and a warm sunshine picnic spot. After making out and making love, you both jumped into the river to cool off and lay back down on the warm blanket in the sunshine.

You fooled around a little too long to catch the outgoing tide. Even Lee had to help paddle the canoe against the incoming tide to get back to the mouth of the river. Any nature lover would die to experience such a peaceful, quiet ride through this wonderland. When you feel stressed or anxious, just remember that peaceful canoeing trip with your dream princess.

She loved that nature trip so much that you took her on a hike up to the Russian Gulch Falls. Always before, your backpack was full of camera equipment. This time, only a bottle of wine and a blanket. The heavy, deep green foliage and fern-covered rocks with the falling water. It reminded her of a trip she had taken back home in the Philippines with her boyfriend. She tried to hide the tears in her eyes as you were sure she was thinking about her boyfriend back home.

You took her to a number of beaches, including the private beach near your old home at Pine Beach. You told her that you had taken some nice nude silhouettes of your first wife on that beach. She started to freak out a little and said she could never do anything like that. You took her to Glass Beach and the private little beaches where you would take those teenage senior portraits. It was much more than the beautiful beaches; it was the pleasant company of your lover. Laughing and talking, we became very good friends, along with being lovers.

You decided to walk the Skunk railroad tracks from town through the redwoods to the company ranch. You showed Lee where you used to hunt ducks behind the Pudding Creek Dam. Remember how frightened she was to walk through the dark Sherwood Road tunnel? It is only about one block long, but it seems much longer.

Come out of the tunnel onto a wooden Trussell over the Noyo River. This is a popular teenage swimming hole, and there were a dozen or so teenagers there that day. Surprised to see two adults walk out of the dark tunnel, they all stopped and stared at you, well, not you, staring at Lee.

The deep pride you felt in yourself for being the one next to such a pretty, sexy girl. All the boys were checking her out, and by the time you crossed the Trussell, their girlfriends were giving them trouble. Somehow, you could tell Lee was also getting into being the center of attention.

You say that because of the way she was flirting with you as the skunk train car passed by. People in the yellow Skunk car were standing to look at her, posing for them with a long kiss as the train went by. She was coming out of her shell and into tight short shorts and bare mid-drift halter tops these days.

One night, you took her out to dinner and danced at the Wharf restaurant down in Noyo Harbor. You tipped the owner and got a window seat just as the sun was setting in the bay. She stared out the window at the fishing boats, and you stared at her lovely face and the cleavage of her beautiful breast in the warm, fading sunset light.

Dancing to the live country band in the lounge was another explosion of new feelings. Now, you had done some slow dancing with several Navy wives between your first wife and your second wife while at school near Lemoore Naval Air Station. The only reason they would ever dance with you was because you were always a gentleman, and other wives had told them so. Let me tell you, those lonely Navy wives did seem to enjoy being held close and tenderly. Navy jet fighter pilots have beautiful wives.

This was going to be a whole new ball game. Dancing with someone else's wife to give her a little fun and comfort as a woman was one thing. Dancing with your lover is a completely different thing. Like not like all the  Navy wives, Lee was not afraid to put her arms around your neck and cuddle her face against your chest. I was not shy about not keeping my hands just on her back and waist. Felt like we moved as a single body together with the music.

It was obvious you were dancing like lovers. In case of any questions, the long, romantic, intimate kiss in the middle of the dance floor settled that question. When the music stopped, you noticed two work buddies and their wives sitting at a table, all staring at you and Lee. Their looks were priceless to you. Given all the earlier problems, you had been involved with them and your first wife.

# Chapter 7

# Yosemite

Lee was enjoying so much all the magnificent nature all around the beautiful North Coast of California. You told her you would like to take her camping high up in the Sierra Navada Mountains in Yosemite National Park. Your dad had an old one-ton 4-wheel drive International Harvester pickup. You had bought a new full-sized overhead camper to go camping with your daughter.

No microwaves or TVs like now. However, it was fully self-contained with a shower and kitchen. The soft, wonderful, full, king-sized bed over the cab of the truck. Water and sewage to last 2 weeks for 2 people.

Lee jumped at the chance and said, Let's go camping. Can I stop off in Stockton to see some family? No problem, sweetie. Will you be her bodyguard or boyfriend at your family, you asked? She just said they were her family; they would be on her side, whatever.

You pulled up in front of the foreman's house in a large group of migrant worker family units. Hardly stopped the camper, and 4 kids piled in through Lee's open window. Tita! Tita! Tita! They were all screaming. The kids escorted you from the camper to the front door. A small crowd had gathered in front of the main house. The men looked like jungle freedom fighters with guns. The women and kids all looked happy to see you.

The door opened, and you instantly became one of the family. They were so happy Lee was safe and enjoying a good time with you. Food, food, and more food. Filipinos really center their social life around food. Wow, what a feast you had in Stockton.

It was crazy how many young, beautiful cousins Lee had at our family dinner table that night. Later, Lee told you they were competing with each other to see who would volunteer for Godfather's backup plan. Backup plan: What backup plan? You know, in case all you wanted was sex and a housekeeper for payment to get her home safe. She told them you were having the time of your life, and her mother had already given you all the money you needed to have a great time.

Lee told you to sit here and watch the kids while she goes shopping for food with her Tita. They went to the Asian store and purchased things they had never heard of, along with special rice cookers and Asian place settings, and cookware. You were about to experience how great a Filipino cook your girlfriend was. Still a long, hot uphill drive from Stockton to Yosemite.

Lee never complained or seemed the least bit uncomfortable in that big, old, noisy truck. In fact, she would lie on the old plastic bench seat and tickle you with her feet. Snuggled up so close and your arm around her for hours. When she needed to cool off, she would hang out the open window and let the wind blow through her thin blouse. Lord, forgive me. I can still see the image of her with the wind blowing against her beautiful female body and the sun shining through that thin white blouse.

When you got to the Yosemite Vista point at the end of the tunnel, you stopped and went to the guardrail to take in the view of Yosemite Valley. Half Dome straight ahead and El Capitan to the left. It is breathtaking. She stood there motionless for a long time, taking in these magnificent works of God, and tears began to roll down her soft face.

Our first stop after that was Bridal Veil Falls. You parked the camper and walked to the viewing area. It was springtime, and the mist from the falls drenched both of you. She began to cry for no reason at all again. You thought it was because people could see she was not wearing a bra, and her beautiful breasts were clinging to her thin white blouse. You asked her why she was crying, and she said she was so happy just being there in that place with you.

You took Lee up the trail to the top of Vernal Falls. It was a good 3-mile hike up from the trailhead to a pool of water just at the top of the falls. When you got there, Lee took off her tube top and hiking shorts and then jumped into the cool pool of water. There were several others on the riverbank and in the pool. When she came out of the water, she looked like a James Bond movie star. Okay, she still had a bra and panties, but Haley Berry had a bikini on too.

You had dinner that first night at the Yosemite Hotel down in the valley. The next few days you spent in the high country of the park. You had been to Yosemite several times before, both backpacking and camping. You parked in a different little hideaway at the end of several dirt roads and trailheads each night. Your dad's old truck, so you did not mind the scratches from the brush or rocks.

That is where she introduced you to some fine Filipino cooking. Her Tita had given her a handwritten bunch of her mother's personal recipes from back home. She said she had watched her mother cook these things, but never had to cook them alone.

Before you left Stockton, they had emptied your camper and filled it with all the Asian cookware and spices that the camper could hold. You learned to like tripe and chicken feet. The chocolate meat was a little too much for you. The way she steamed those rice balls and all the dim sum dishes she could think of. So many strange and wonderful dishes you never thought possible.

Your senses were all on overload. Everything seemed to be so right. Sitting by a high mountain stream, holding hands, watching the birds fly by. Viewing Yosemite Falls this time of snow melt is awesome. So at peace with God and have such a sweet soulmate to share it all with.

Not just the fact that she was so fantastically beautiful, but she was really enjoying the very same things you had such affection for. Yosemite will always be your favorite place in this whole world, and Lee loved it just as much.

Sitting in those peaceful, quiet places with such a sweet lover was so great to remember. I don't remember any specific place or conversation, but I do remember there were several places where we held hands and just listened to nature for long periods of time. Sometimes, only to break and start watching her read her mother's recipes and prepare another meal to die for.

To look at such glory in God's creation and in the midst of all that beauty, God's most beautiful creation of all was Lee. So sweet and good-natured. So much fun to be with all day, with much less to wake up with after a night of cuddling and making out. Camping with her was like camping with a goddess, and she can cook too.

On your way out of Yosemite, you stopped to pray next to the chapel in Yosemite Valley. Both of you cried after praying. Without saying a word to each other, we knew our prayers were not the same. It was as close to heaven as you will ever be in this world.

Yosemite changed your relationship with Lee to a spiritual level, and you both knew it. You were sure she was coming to the same level as you. It was in Yosemite that you were truly at peace with your princess. Both of you were also at peace with God in Yosemite. You played together like you were kids, laughing all night and touching each other. Wake up with her, together, all the beauty of nature all around you.

# Chapter 8

# Juan Creek Beach

You thought nothing could possibly top the experience of camping in Yosemite with Lee. Hold on, your fantasy dream was about to come true.

After Yosemite, you took Lee camping on a secluded private beach several miles north of town. You had been working for the power company for several years, plus you had lived here all your life until after your first marriage. You knew a locked gate south of Juan Creek that led to a tiny private campsite next to the beach. You unlocked the gate with your power company passkey and backed the camper down the narrow dirt brush-covered road. A level spot just big enough for your camper and a rock fire pit right at the edge of the sand.

You had seen that secluded beach when patrolling the power lines. You also knew that if anyone would park at the highway turnout high above and walk a short distance, they could look over the steep bluff at the ocean and see the small white beach below. Did not tell Lee that.

Now it was getting closer to the date you were supposed to deliver her to the airport. Lee was pulling out all the stops now to convince you to marry her. She was willing to do just about anything, so you sweetly talked her into posing nude for you on that beach.

You promised to give her all the films so she would be the only one to ever see them. You also promised that her granddaughters would love to see how beautiful their Lola was when she was young.

"Why would you do that and give me all the film?" she asked. It has been my fantasy to photograph such a perfect figure and form of a woman. Always before, there were imperfections to avoid. The joy of photographing you will be payment in full, even if I never see them. Besides the memory of shooting you, it will last you a lifetime.

You did not bring your medium format camera, but you just happened to have some rolls of Kodachrome and your Canon 35mm. Back in the camper were your Norman Studio battery power pack, strobe lights, stands, and umbrella light reflectors.

The first session was at sunset that first night. You had taken a number of nude silhouette sunset photos before. All earlier shoots were extremely stressful and very demanding. Taking pleasing photos of girls was always easy and natural for you. Photographing nude girls is a whole new experience. The worry about camera angles and position to hide or reduce flaws and imperfections is much harder without clothes.

No such thing with Lee. She was shy and sat perfectly still as she let you position and re-position her over and over. Along with her high, firm, perfectly shaped, generous breast, her long, thin arms and legs made one classic silhouetted pose after another. No tricks needed to idealize this female form. Although she was a tiny little woman, her body proportions were classic. Relatively long, slender, beautiful, shaped legs and arms, and the grace to frame herself against the setting sun.

You shot several exposures of Kodachrome that sunset with the most magnificent female body in front of the most beautiful sunset of your life. In your old age, you should be reminded how wonderful that photo session made you feel. Kodachrome was very unforgiving of exposure. Sunset silhouettes are very hard to get the exposure just right. I hope I did okay.

The second session was midday the next day. You had your white umbrellas and strobe lights with a battery power pack and stands all set up to fill the shadows of the midday sun. You also needed the bright sun to light up the dark blue ocean and sky in the background. This is old-school film photography. No digital post session Photoshop here. The actual set had to be the final product.

Then Lee hands you her towel and steps into the set. You thought the sunset silhouettes blew your mind.

Lee was way more relaxed this time. So much more, she began to make love to your camera. They were way more intimate and romantic than you thought this shy little goddess could give you. If her granddaughters ever get to look at these pictures of grandma, they will not have to ask if she was having sex with the photographer. There was that much sensuality in every shot.

She must have figured out you would be asking her to pose for you. She must have done some reading or something. Whatever, she was posing without direction from you, from one great pose to the next. The intimate look in her eyes and long dark hair flowing in the sea breeze. She was acting like a professional model with one sensual look after another.

It was difficult to maintain focus on all the points of interest of your model. Naturally, everyone would be mesmerized by the ancient Greek statue of a figure. Her high, firm, generous pair of breasts and tiny waist. Those thin firm thighs and athletic butt. You kept clicking the shutter, but all you were really looking at was her captivating Asian eyes.

Trying to keep her focused on being your model and not your lover was difficult. She had her father's Japanese almond-shaped eyes and her mother's beautiful little Filipino nose and full lips. Soft white Japanese skin, a Filipino smile, and a pleasing nature.

Lee became so comfortable with you that she became more natural, and she gave you such an innocent look. One classic pose after another to show off such a perfect body. Everyone had sensual and pleasant expressions. Then she started to laugh about something and gave you a lot of smiling, happy, and fun shots.

It was not all happening on the beach. What was going on in the camper was pretty special, too. Not just the sex and sleeping together, it was the laughing and playing around in the camper. You danced to every Fleetwood Mac and Eagles song you had on the boombox. The slow dancing on that tiny camper floor with Lee barely dressed, cuddled next to you. She had learned how to slink around like a viper, sending shock waves up and down your spine. Lee had turned into a real vixen at Juan Creek Beach.

I still have the image of her cooking food at that camper stove for you to remember. She is standing in front of the open camper door with the waves crashing on the beach outside just behind her. We were so close to the waves crashing on the beach that we had to raise the volume on the music. She is wearing a thin white T-shirt with the sunlight showing off her female body underneath. Lee cooked you some great Filipino food in that little camper.

Writing about this brings back memories of some great times sharing meals with your little princess. Always so cheerful and happy and so nice to be around. She was always telling you Filipino jokes and pulling tricks on you. Waking up in the morning with this angel, looking out the camper window at that secluded private California beach, what a time to remember.

Then your final night at the beach came around way too soon. It was time to tell her one last time that you had made your decision not to marry her. It was your responsibility to deliver her to the airport so she could go home and marry the true love of her life. You would trust God to deliver her safely in Manila and forget about getting married and living together for two years. It was all over for you, and it was time to go back home.

That was a night to forget. Crying most of the night. In the morning, you had your last photo session with her on the beach. It was cold and foggy, and her mood was very solemn and thoughtful. It went well with the soft grey, even natural ambient light of the fog.

There were not so many smiles this morning, but mostly gentle eyes staring off into the distance. There were no nude poses that day, but lots of soft, smooth skin and so very pleasant amounts of cleavage to show off those beautiful breasts. The goose bumps from the cold wind added just the right touch to her soft Asian skin.

Today, more than ever, her lovely Filipino hands were telling stories like an old-fashioned Filipino dancer. Telling stories with her hands and long, shapely arms forming lines of interest to enhance her figure in every frame.

That very private week on that secluded beach with your princess of your dreams will be the highlight of your passion for photography. Think about all the pictures you took of so many drop-dead gorgeous girls and the thousands of other things you love to photograph.

Nothing ever came close to the feeling you enjoyed that week with your Playboy model on the beach and in your camper. You have always dreamed of being a playboy or a Sports Illustrated swimsuit photographer. For you, this was a boyhood fantasy dream come true.

You knew it was hard to keep from getting emotional and starting to cry all over again. I hope you were able to catch all that emotion in those sensual last photos.

Tomorrow we will be breaking camp and will be taking you to the airport to go home. One last night at your parents' house to wash clothes and pack for her trip back home. Your heart was breaking inside, but you were afraid to let it show. Lee made it very clear that her heart was breaking, too.

All the plans and all the big talk, but nobody planned to fall in love like you did. Just the time I needed God's help, her mother provided just what I needed to be strong enough to put your love aside and go through with it.

One last phone call to the Philippines to find out things were getting much better back home. The whole family had moved back to Manila, and it was now safe for Lee to come home again. Lee talked for a very long and emotional time, talking to her mom. She let you talk to her so she could thank you for being so nice to her daughter. She said she was missing Lee so much and was really looking forward to her coming home. She slipped up and mentioned that her boyfriend had stopped by and could not wait to hold her in his arms again.

Lee confessed that she was in turmoil inside about her boyfriend. That phone call from Mom was the final confirmation for you. No matter how much it hurt, no matter the tears it was going to cause, it was the right thing to do. Lee deserved so much better than this old country boy. She deserved the good life waiting for her back home, no matter how it may break her heart to say goodbye to you.

# Chapter 9

# Taking Her to the Airport

The most fantastic month of your life came to a sad ending. It was time to take Lee to the airport. Watching her say goodbye to your folks was much harder than you thought possible. With what little time you allowed them to be together, they still grew a great attachment to each other. She saw where you got your soft emotional side from. Your dad cried and shook like a baby as he hugged Lee goodbye.

You had planned for several days to stop at Hendy Wood State Park on the way to the airport. It had been a very emotional and sad 2-hour drive from home to your favorite stand of old-growth redwood trees. During your darkest times, you prayed in that holy cathedral under that canopy of the tallest trees on earth.

You walked from the car, gently holding her tiny hand as you entered this holy place. Walking out of the bright sunlight into the dim shadows under the trees. Shafts of sunlight coming through those tall trees. The awesome strength you feel looking at those giant redwood trees, massive trunks all around you, reaching up to the sky.

The green ferns and clover, with tiny purple flowers that cover the ground, are such a quiet, surreal environment. I always think of this as God's Holy Cathedral in the redwoods just for you.

You took her to a place you had been before, next to the tallest tree in the grove.

Just like in Yosemite, the spirit of God came over both of you. You both opened your hearts out to God and prayed out loud, just like the three of you were sitting there together. Lee thanked Jesus in front of you for the wonderful time He had given her with you. She also thanked Him for the sweet and gentle love He gave her to bring her back home safe.

You thanked Jesus for the precious gift of love you could feel from Lee. You prayed He would give her comfort and peace as you must soon part. Then you both asked Jesus to forgive you for the unholy sins that you had committed together in the name of love.

A great peace fell over both of you, and then you put your arms around her, and you both cried for a very long time, still on your knees. All these years later, I see God is still answering our prayers, that somehow God has forgiven our sins, and our spirits will always be together.

You got a motel room at the Oakland airport for her to catch her early morning flight back home to the Philippines. You met the man from the foreign bride agency and gave him the money Lee had given you to cover the agreement. You went back to the cold, dark motel room to spend your last night together.

It was such an emotionally sad night for both of you. You lie in bed holding each other. You knew it would be your last night on earth together. You kissed and cried all night long. In the height of her emotional pain, she offered herself to you for the first time. It broke your heart to know her love for you was that real. You had no choice except to break her heart even as she cried. She would be going home an unspoiled virgin in the morning.

Deep down in the back of your mind, you always wondered if she was only acting all along. If she was, she was damn good at it. To go so far as to even offer herself, I knew her love was real.

In the morning, there was a knock at the door. A tall Filipino man dressed in the formal white barong asked if Lee was here. I asked him in, and when Lee saw him, her eyes lit up. She ran to him, and they hugged each other like family. It was her godfather's personal bodyguard. Lee knew him well from visits with her godfather. He handed me a short note. Thank you for protecting my little girl.

I asked the man if he was going to fly home with Lee. He just nodded yes. As I turned to Lee, time stood still. The moment of goodbye has come for us. I turned to the man and asked if he could please wait here in the motel room with her until she was ready to go to the terminal. Again, he just nodded yes.

You prayed silently to God for the strength to do what you knew to be His will. You slowly turned back to Lee, just about to start crying. You gave her a small nod and pointed to the bodyguard with your puckered lips. The Filipino way, just like she had taught you to.

So as not to show any affection in front of "Mr. T," You simply kissed her hand and said goodbye, Princess. You turned and walked out the door. Never to see her again. Then you went to the observation deck to watch her plane take off. You felt both of your hearts break as it lifted off. Never to feel her soft, moist lips again.

**Life After Lee**

That was the end of my story five years ago.

Now I'm not so sure if Lee was real or just someone I made up. You have no proof that this story is true. For all you know, Lee could have been just a pretty poor little girl from the province. Caught up in a very bad human trafficking situation out of desperation. The money you received could have come from her family and friends in the province, just desperately trying to keep her safe and to get her back home.

Real or fantasy, wealthy or poor, you knew how smart she was at telling you stories. I would have believed her if she had told me she was an alien from another planet.

It's up to the reader of this story to decide. She was way too good to be true.

However, if she were real, what a pleasant, romantic escapade she had with her American secret gentleman lover.

64

# Chapter 10

# Addendum to My Fantasy Princess

# Apong babae
## (Tagalog for Granddaughter)

To My Fantasy Princess' Granddaughter (apong babae)

This is a letter that could be to any aging Filipina lady suffering from a loss of her memory. A few years ago, I wrote a short story about a beautiful young Filipina lady. It was half-truth and half fantasy back in the 1980s. I gave the story the name "My Fantasy Princess". After reading that story, it was clear that I was my princess's playmate and not the other way around.

I don't really know if the lady in my Fantasy Princess story exists or not. No matter, she could be your grandmother if she could just pretend to be my princess in my story while you read her the story of her California lover. It might make her feel young and beautiful and alive again for an hour.

Go visit your grandmother and ask her if you can read her a story that could be about her. If she is willing, read her my story, "My Fantasy Princess." If she liked it, tell her you have some more personal information about her make-believe relationship with the photographer.

Or the next time you visit her, you can tell her you received a letter from me. My letter would read…

Hello, my little apong babae.

I got your message asking for more information about a photograph you found in your mother's things.

This is a letter from the man taking the photographs of your beautiful Lola many years ago. First of all, your Lola was a lady. She was not only beautiful on the outside, but she was also full of grace and laughter on the inside.

If you read the story about my Fantasy Princess, you will learn about all the wonderful things we did and the places we went together. The things I say in this letter are much deeper and more from my heart.

You can read about the brave and scary things she did because she loved her Nanay and Tatay so much. We had a contest to see who had the very best childhood. Read me my story about my first foster home and see just what a wonderful childhood I had.

The stories she told me about her Nanay and Tatay won the contest.

You and Lola, and I were more than just lovers. We shared so many stories about each other's lives. She put her sweet arms around me and cried when I told her about how I lost my foster daughter, Pam.

Then she cheered me up, telling me another story about sailing with her godfather. She told the story to make me believe I was really on his yacht watching the sunset with her lovers' arms around her.

Yes, we were lovers sleeping together every night. You already know we had a sexual relationship. You may not know that Lola and I had a spiritual relationship, also. How close to God we came when we were in Yosemite.

Praying down by the Yosemite Valley chapel with her was something so special. Praying with her in the redwood grove was more like a visit to heaven itself.

The three of us, all sitting there together by that giant redwood tree. Holding hands in both body and spirit with your Lola, together with the HOLY SPIRIT, was such a glorious experience.

I can still see her dancing to the country music in that camper on the beach in her nightshirt. She was so sexy and playful all the time. She always had a big smile on her beautiful lips. The emotion in her sweet voice as she sang her Tagalog love songs was so beautiful to me. I felt like I was a private audience of one listening to a nightingale sing.

I don't know what picture she showed you. She was so frightened by the first sunset beach nude silhouettes, then so sexy and exciting for the beach nude photos. Her sadness on our last day on the beach.

Whatever photo you are looking at with her. Please tell her what a joy and privilege it was to be trusted so deeply to be her cameraman.

She had to follow the path that God had made for her, and so did I. It took the strength of the mighty God to allow us the power to part.

I know she doesn't remember now, but she was in love. It was breaking her already broken heart to say goodbye to me just as much as it was breaking mine. Your precious Lola blessed me with a month of her life. Please hug her and tell her I still love her.

Please tell her how much I long to give her my holy embrace in heaven when we all get there. She can re-live that crazy month and feel like the sexy, beautiful woman she still is inside.

The most important thing I wish to tell you about your Lola. Even on the way back in Disneyland, your Lola told me how much in love she was with her boyfriend back home. I don't have any question that she is still in love with him today, as I am still in love with all my ex-wives all these years later.

That month we shared together was only our fantasies. A private piece of both of our lives that has nothing to do with our love for both of our spouses. Please tell your Lolo how much your Lola has always loved him.

With all my Love, your Lola's secret lover.

Maybe you have a Lola in a home somewhere, like my princess. Read her my story and let her pretend she is the princess in the story. My prayer would be that it would make her feel young and beautiful again and let her see how wonderful God's love for her really is.

Your Lola may not remember just how close she was walking with GOD even during this unholy fling with an old redneck hippy back in California. I can testify she had the time of her life, and so did I. I am so grateful to GOD for the month I was able to share with your precious Lola.

Like in the movie, "The Notebook," if only for a few minutes, she can be on that beach again with the waves reflecting her beautiful body in the warm surf sunset.

The End.

www.ingramcontent.com/pod-product-compliance
Lightning Source LLC
Chambersburg PA
CBHW070655010826
48975CB00013B/1298